D0633689

Nicholas Bentley Stoningpot III

Nicholas Bentley Stoningpot III

by Ann McGovern

illustrated by Tomie de Paola

Holiday House New York

Printed in the United States of America
First Edition

Library of Congress Cataloging in Publication Data

McGovern, Ann.
Nicholas Bentley Stoningpot III.

SUMMARY: A bored little rich boy is shipwrecked on a faraway island where he is happier than he has ever been before.
[1. Shipwrecks—Fiction. 2. Islands—Fiction] I. De Paola, Tomie, ill. II. Title.
PZ7.M1687Ni [E] 81-13226
ISBN 0-8234-0443-9 AACR2

For Marty, who shares a paradise island
A. McG.

For Lon Driggers, who was preppy when I first met him and now has his private paradise on top of a hill
T. deP.

Nicholas Bentley Stoningpot III was sailing the seas on a beautiful boat with his parents and their friends. All day, Nicky listened to the clink of their drinks.

His mother said, "Do you know what the baron said to the countess?"

His father said, "Did you hear what the duke did?"

And on and on and on.

The cook made Nicky special treats he could not eat. The butler brought Nicky fancy drinks he could not swallow.

The crew did exciting things. But Nicky was not allowed to be with them.

At night, they played games and told funny stories.

But Nicky had to be in bed by seven o'clock.

Nicky was bored.

"I am bored, bored, bored," he shouted to the wind.
"Bored, bored, bored," he called to the white sea birds.

"Bored, bored, bored," he cried to his parents.

But they didn't hear him over the clink of their drinks and the patter of their chatter.

Nicky longed for adventure. "Any little adventure will do," he sobbed into his satin pillowcase.

That night the wind howled. The waves tossed. The thunder cracked. The lightning lit and split the skies.

SMACK. CRACK. POW.

The big boat was sinking in the storm. The adults grabbed their diamonds and furs, and the crew sailed them away to safety in the lifeboat.

The big beautiful boat smashed to pieces. And Nicky was adrift on a piece of the smashed boat. For two days and two nights, he drifted. He was cold and wet and hungry and thirsty. And he was not alone. Big sharks and big whales swam around and around him.

On the morning of the third day, Nicky was almost a goner. He opened his eyes to take a last look at the world. What did he see but land! Beautiful land! He saw an island ringed with trees and fringed by a white, sandy beach.

It was perfect.

"I'll call my island Monkey Island," Nicky said. "In honor of my new friend."

Nicky had plenty to eat—fresh fish every day and wild nuts and berries and fruit. He had plenty to drink—fresh goat's milk and coconut milk. He had plenty to do. He made a little house. He made a bed, a table, and two chairs. One chair was for the monkey. He made plates and a glass and a toothbrush.

He made a sign on the highest part of the island:

Nicky had never been so happy in all of his life.

Meanwhile, 5,000 miles away, his parents discovered he was missing. Headlines in the newspapers read:

The Daily Sun

BILLIONAIRE'S SON LOST AT SEA
ONE MILLION-DOLLAR REWARD FOR
NICHOLAS BENTLEY STONINGPOT III

Helicopters flew the skies looking for him. Boats roamed the seas searching for him.

And on faraway Monkey Island, Nicky found a new delight in every day.

The storm that shipwrecked Nicky wrecked other ships, too. Some of the drifting cargo made its way toward Monkey Island.

Every day, new treasures washed up on the shore. Three pairs of shoes and tattered clothes. Old feather hats and funny wigs. One day Nicky found a trunk—filled with games and books and chocolate bars.

He collected piles of treasure. Nicky grew strong from his healthy outdoor life. He grew smart from reading hard books.

One morning Nicky was awakened by shrieking parrots and crying goats. The monkey was howling and running up and down the trees. The reason for the commotion was a rescue boat, sailing closer and closer to Monkey Island.

But Nicky didn't want to be rescued. He wanted to stay right where he was—on this island, with the parrots and the goats and the monkey. Quickly he searched through his pile of treasure. He made a wonderful disguise.

Now he didn't look a bit like Nicholas Bentley Stoningpot III. He looked like a gray-haired old lady.

The rescuers peered through their telescopes.

"There's no one on that island but a monkey, two goats, and a gray-haired old lady," they said, and they sailed away.

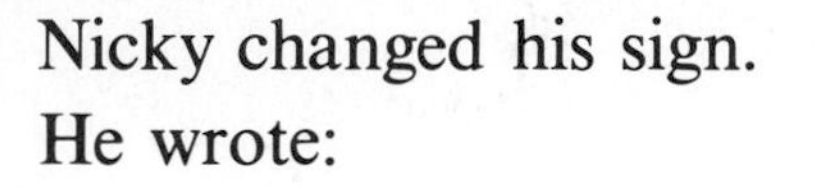

Nicky changed his sign.
He wrote:

Whenever Nicky heard rescue planes in the sky or saw rescue boats in the sea, he dipped into his pile of treasure.

He fooled them all. Some days he looked like a mean, fierce pirate.

Some days he looked like a clown.

Once he looked like a wild beast.
No one thought he looked like Nicholas Bentley Stoningpot III.

After awhile, the newspapers got tired of printing stories of the billionaire's missing son. Nicky's parents spent the million-dollar reward on more diamonds and furs and another big beautiful boat.

Nicky was very happy on his island. Every day, he had new adventures. He made a fine, strong raft for sailing away. He thought one day he might want to leave Monkey Island, and go back to the real world.

But not yet.
Not for a long, long time.